Nature Quest

Text: Corinne Delporte
Illustrations: Nelvana Ltd

CRACKBOOM!

Today is Earth Day, and everybody is getting ready to celebrate in Big Sky Park. Mom calls Rob to wake him up.

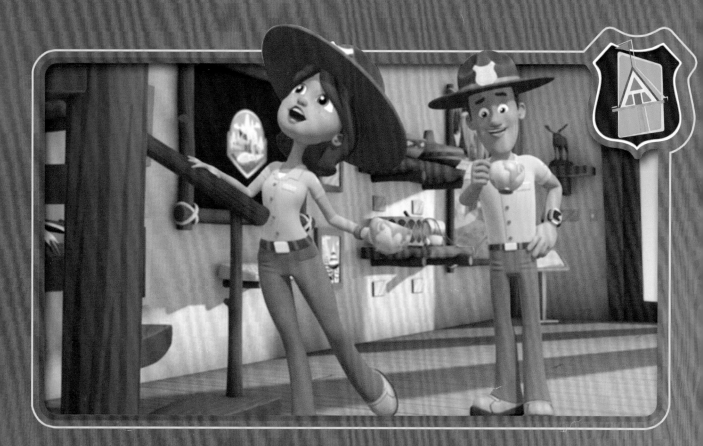

"Rob, time to get up, it's Earth D—"
"Earth Day!" says Rob, as he bursts into the house.
Rob is already up and dressed. He is more eager to celebrate Earth Day than anyone else.

"I've already washed Chipper, emptied the recycling bin and raked the leaves. I don't want to miss a minute of the Earth Day celebrations."

Mom and Dad are really impressed by Rob.

What am I waiting for?

Ranger Rob puts on his ranger outfit.

RANGER HAT

BANDOLIER KIT

ROB is ranger ready to get outside!

He speeds over the forest on a zipline.

Then he calls
CHIPPER, his high-tech
all-terrain vehicle, and jumps in.

He is quickly joined by his
best friend **STOMPER**
the yeti.

Hey, hey, where are we going today?

To the
forest!

says Ranger Rob, as they soar high in the sky.

Ranger Rob and Stomper land in front of the Ranger Station and welcome Dakota, Sam and the visitors. They all sing and dance and decorate the Ranger Station together.

It's Earth Day, it's Earth Day in Big Sky Park!
It's Earth Day, it's Earth Day,
Come and join the Celebrations!

"Happy Earth Day!" says Mom.
"To celebrate this day, we give a special present to Big Sky Park. This year, the Jungle Restaurant is getting new rain barrels."

The crowd claps happily.

"Today, think of the things nature can help us do."
"We can use the wind to surf on the snow," says Stomper.

"Or the sun to power solar cars in the desert," adds Sam.

"And what will we do at the end of the day?" asks Mom.
"We will plant an Earth Day tree and have a party under the stars!"
answers Rob.

Hooray!

Just then the solarcopter appears in the sky. It is Big Sky Park's brand-new helicopter. Its first mission will be to carry a tree that needs to be saved and take it back to the Ranger Station to be planted.

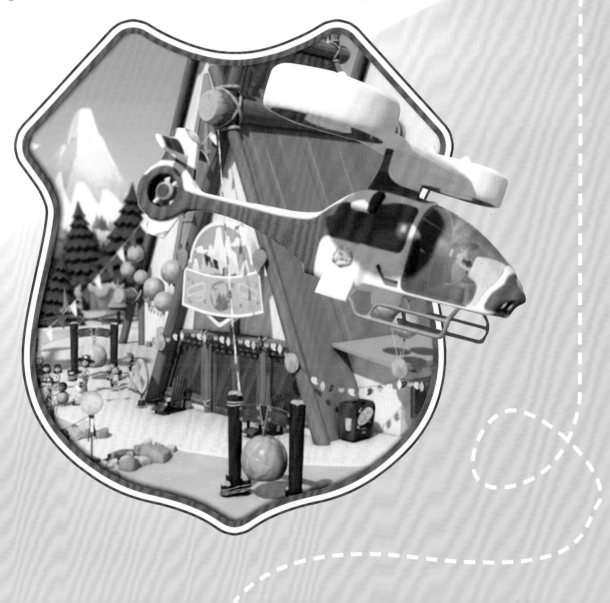

Mom sends Rob and his friends on a Nature Quest. They will have to move the rain barrels from the jungle clearing to the Jungle Restaurant.

WOO-hoo, let's go! says ROB.

And they all run to the river together.

"Here are the barrels," says Rob.
Sam is worried.
"But the restaurant is on the other side of the jungle. How do we get the rain barrels all the way over there?"

Rob has an idea.

"We'll use water power. The natural flow of the water will carry the barrels to the Jungle Restaurant."

Rob and his friends put the barrels in the water and jump into them. "We will go on a jungle tour at the same time!" exclaims Dakota.

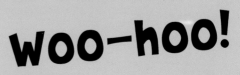

NATURE QUEST ACCOMPLISHED!

says Rob.

Rob and his friends reach the shore. Thanks to some great team work, it doesn't take long to deliver the barrels to the restaurant.

"What will these barrels be used for?" asks Sam.
Rob explains that they will collect rainwater to wash
dishes for example. This will save water.
"Let's go to the Frosty Fields!" says Rob.

Ranger Rob and his friends jump onto their windsurf boards.
"The wind is really making us go," Dakota says.

Yay, wind power!

As they glide over the snow, they are joined by
penguins who race with them, sliding on their bellies.

The sun is high in the sky. Sam tells his friends that now is the best time to drive solar cars.
"To the desert!" says Sam.

woo-hoo!

yay,
solar
Power!

After a fun-filled day, Ranger Rob and his friends go back to the Ranger Station.

"Today, we used water, wind and solar power. Awesome!" says Dakota. "A good ranger can find all kinds of power in nature," says Rob.

Sniff, Sniff!

"My yeti snifferoo is picking up a smell. A good smell!"
Stomper runs toward Woolly, and his friends follow.
"Mmm, a delicious Earth Day marmalade. My favorite!"
"Thank you, cousin. I will bring a jar for everyone at the
starlight party tonight," says Woolly. "Happy Earth Day!"

Rob and his friends arrive at the Ranger Station just in time. Night has fallen and the stars are sparkling in the sky. Everyone is ready for the starlight party.

The solarcopter is back with the giant tree. With Chipper's help,
Rob and his friends plant the tree.
"Do the cheer, Rob!" asks one of the visitors.
"Okay! When I say 'Big Sky,' you say 'Park.' Big Sky . . ."
"PARK!" answers the crowd.

HAPPY Earth Day!

CrackBoom! Books is an imprint of Chouette Publishing (1987) Inc.

Text: adaptation by Corinne Delporte of the animated series Ranger Rob, produced by Nelvana
Limited/Ranger Rob UK Limited.
All rights reserved.
Original script written by Carolyn Hay and Andrew Sabiston
Original episode #117: Earth Day in Big Sky Park
Illustrations: Nelvana Ltd

 Ranger Rob is a trademark of Nelvana Limited. All Rights Reserved.

Chouette Publishing would like to thank the Government of Canada and SODEC
for their financial support.

Books
Tax Credit

Québec
Gestion
SODEC

Bibliothèque et Archives nationales du Québec and Library and Archives Canada
cataloguing in publication

Delporte, Corinne

[Mission nature. English]

Nature quest/adaptation, Corinne Delporte; illustrations, Nelvana Ltd.

(Ranger Rob)
Translation of: Mission nature.
Target audience: For children aged 3 and up.

ISBN 978-2-924786-41-3 (softcover)

I. Nelvana (Firm), illustrator. II. Title. III. Title: Mission nature. English.

PZ7.1.D44Na 2018   j843'.92   C2017-942600-1

Printed in Canada
10 9 8 7 6 5 4 3 2 1 CHO2029 MAR2018

MIX
Paper from
responsible sources
FSC® C103304